april pulley sayre
with jeff sayre

Warbler Wave

beach lane books • new york
london   toronto   sydney   new delhi

In spring, as you nightly nap,
warblers flap
over oceans, lakes,
and mountains.

Tiny. Strong.
Pushed along
by wings
and rivers of wind.

They share
the air
with buildings,
bats, turbines, and towers.

Then bedraggled, they drop.
A refueling stop.
They must find food
or die.

They search. Stalk.

Wag. Walk.

So dainty,
these colorful diners.

Yellow.

Blue.

Pattern.

Hue.

They flit, like flying flowers.

They look.

Lean.

Grab. Glean.

Crushers of caterpillars!
Slurpers of spiders!

They flutter. Catch.
Sally. Snatch.

Check cracks,

leaf backs.

Climb ridges.

Energy ebbs?
Check the webs—

for mosquitoes,

moths,

and midges!

Warblers sing.

Preen.

Scan the local scene.

Owls nap.

Woodchucks chew.

But there's no more time to rest.

It's north to nest!

After dusk,
warblers rise to fly.

They call in the night.
Keep in touch while in flight.

Surfing rivers of wind way up high . . .

calling *zeep, zeep, zeep* in the sky.

A Migration Marathon

Warblers are tiny songbirds. About 50 species of warblers are regularly seen in the United States and Canada. Most weigh half an ounce or less—as much as two baby carrots or three nickel coins. Yet every year many of these petite athletes migrate hundreds, even thousands, of miles.

The migrants spend late fall, winter, and early spring in Mexico, Central America, South America, the Caribbean islands, or the southeastern United States. Then they travel north to the mainland United States, Alaska, or Canada. Their migration is a marathon. How far a bird flies each night depends on its energy reserves and the weather. Storms and winds may push them off the direct route. A headwind—wind blowing toward them—may slow them down.

Over Land and Sea

To travel north from South America, some birds fly over land, above Central America and Mexico. Others follow a more direct route, straight over the Gulf of Mexico. This part of the trip may require a single long night and a tailwind—wind pushing the bird in the direction it needs to go. Tired birds sometimes land on oil rigs and boats out in the Gulf in order to rest. Many migrating birds just barely make it to land.

Why Migrate?

Why do most warblers fly north in spring to nest, then return south in fall? Scientists' best guess is insects and nesting space. Northern forests are rich in insects during spring and summer. Summer days in the north have more hours of daylight than down south where the birds winter. This allows warblers extra hours each day to hunt insects in order to feed their growing young. Also, there is less competition for food and nesting space than in the tropics.

While feeding their families, warblers and other migrating songbirds provide a service to the forest. Just imagine how many insects migrating birds (and migrating bats, for that matter) eat. If the birds were not there to eat the caterpillars, the caterpillars, in much larger numbers, might be dining on leafy trees. Would that have an impact on tree health? The answer needs study.

It's an Instinct

The urge to migrate is an instinct. Even if kept indoors, with no changes in light or temperature, birds experience *Zugunruhe* (ZOO-guhn-roo-uh). This is migratory restlessness. They gain weight to store energy for their journey. They begin to hop and flutter in the direction they should migrate.

Finding Their Way

No one gives warblers a map. And they do not learn the route from their parents, as geese do. Warblers hatch with the instinct to fly in a certain direction during migration. Researchers think the birds can sense—perhaps even see with their eyes—the earth's magnetic field. They can navigate by stars and the direction of the setting sun.

On their second migration, they know their route better. So they can navigate by incorporating landmarks as well. They may hear ocean waves crash on shore. They are so good at navigating that most can find their way even if they are blown off course.

Tracking the Migration

How do scientists know birds migrate? Much of the evidence comes from birdwatchers' observations and bird banding—catching and releasing birds that have been fitted with tiny numbered anklets. Bird banders sometimes catch the same bird they have banded during previous journeys.

Scientists—and birdwatchers—also learn about migration through Doppler weather radar. At times, there are so many birds migrating that they can be seen on weather radar. The radar bounces off the birds' bodies. Speckles appear on the radar and shift outward as the mass of birds takes off or lands.

Recently, scientists fitted Kirtland's warblers with tiny backpacks that can sense differences in light levels. The backpacks record the times of sunrise and sunset and other light cues to figure out the bird's location every day during migration. The backpacks do not transmit this data to scientists. (Current technology that transmits is heavier, and more of a burden for a migrating bird.) Instead, the scientists must recapture the bird to retrieve the data from the previous year.

Rivers of Wind

Migrating birds power their way through their journey by flapping their wings. But they also catch rides on air currents—rivers of wind up in the sky. These currents push birds, carrying them at faster speeds and shortening the journey. Airplanes sometimes take advantage of such currents too, but jets mostly fly much higher in the sky than warblers. Songbirds such as warblers do much of their migrating at 500–2,000 feet above the ground, although some have been recorded flying higher.

The Blackpoll's Remarkable Journey

Scientist William V. DeLuca and his team tracked blackpoll warblers. Each year these birds fly about 4,000 miles round trip during migration. Before the fall migration, the birds fatten up. Then their intestines shrink, saving weight and energy for the journey.

They won't be eating for several days anyway, because they fly for three days, nonstop. They head out over the Atlantic Ocean, far offshore, catch winds south, and land in Puerto Rico or on other Caribbean islands to rest and feed before moving onward to Venezuela and Colombia. After landing, their intestines plump up and regrow. But it can take several days before they can fully digest food and gather energy to journey onward.

Stopovers for Survival

Once over land, warblers may stop to rest and feed almost anywhere, from a tiny park in Iowa to a schoolyard in Kentucky. You may see them in Central Park in New York City, in downtown Atlanta, or in small shrubs on Chicago's lakeshore.

Certain lake edges and ocean shores tend to host more warblers because birds may stop to rest before crossing large areas of water. Or they may skirt the water, traveling in shorter flights along the shorelines.

A Change of Scene

Imagine a small bird arriving in a new place for a stopover. Only a few weeks earlier, it was zooming past iguanas on sunny Caribbean islands. Or it may have been sipping irrigation water in a chili pepper field in Mexico. It could have been flitting around a coffee plantation in Costa Rica or above monkeys in a cloud forest in Ecuador.

Now imagine being a resident animal or birdwatcher when the warblers arrive in spring! The warblers' bright colors flash as they zig and zag through the trees, and their songs layer and intertwine with the *tap-tap* of woodpeckers and the chirps of chickadees and all the other birds that stay year-round. It's like a little bit of the tropical rain forest or the Caribbean islands has come to visit. Birdwatchers embrace the challenge of trying to see, listen to, and photograph these colorful, quick-moving visitors.

Awesome Insectivores

Warblers often "glean" their prey, picking aphids, caterpillars, and other tiny insects from the surfaces of leaves, twigs, and tree trunks. To hunt flying insects, warblers sally—quickly swoop out, then return to their perch. They also flutter among leaves or in front of spiderwebs. They probe flowers and crevices for hidden insects.

Hungry Visitors

"Bird fat is fuel in a bird's migration engine," says Kimberly Kaufman, executive director of the Black Swamp Bird Observatory. "Many migrating warblers will double their body weight eating insects to build up the fat stores they need to power their migration."

The timing of warbler migration and the availability of certain food sources is important. Midges hatch on Lake Erie in early May, right near the peak of warbler migration. Near Chicago, white oak tree leaves emerge right when migrating warblers arrive and the birds feed on caterpillars among the tiny leaves. In the fall, elderberry bushes in the Midwest produce fruit at the right time to feed birds migrating south. Wax myrtle bushes in the Southeast provide berries that yellow-rumped warblers can eat in winter.

Warblers: Beautiful Blurs

Warblers are some of the most beautiful birds on earth. But they are small and fast-moving, so it takes practice to find them and identify them.

The challenge of finding warblers is actually part of the excitement and fun of seeing them. Young people interested in seeing warblers and other birds are sharing their interest through groups like the Ohio Young Birders Club and similar youth organizations in other states, as well as through national youth birding camp programs.

Listen for Their Night Calls

Small birds such as warblers migrate at night because the air is cooler and they are less likely to overheat as they work hard to fly. They can also avoid daytime predators such as hawks.

On a quiet night, you may hear warblers calling as they travel overhead. Researcher Bill Evans tracks migrating birds by their night flight calls. He points a microphone at the sky to hear them and has learned to identify their calls. To find out more about bird calls, consult the Cornell Lab of Ornithology: birds.cornell.edu.

Warbler Hot Spots

During migration, warblers tend to stop at some of the same sites, year after year. Between mid-April and mid-May, the following sites are considered "warbler hot spots"—places where tired birds often rest in large numbers: Cape May, New Jersey; Ottawa National Wildlife Refuge and Magee Marsh Wildlife Area, Ohio; Point Pelee, Ontario, Canada; Dauphin Island, Alabama; South Padre Island, Texas; and the Dry Tortugas, Florida.

Welcoming the Guests

Wherever you live, you can help migrating birds. The most important thing you can do is provide them with habitat. A habitat is a safe place that contains food, water, shelter, and, if needed, a place to raise young. Migrating birds need winter habitat, summer habitat, and rest stop habitats along their journey. Ask a local nature center, birding club, or Audubon Society about projects that protect and improve local bird habitat. Here are some habitat-helping tips to keep in mind:

Food: Warblers rarely come to bird feeders. They eat insects, spiders, and berries. So the best bird feeders for them are trees, bushes, and vines that have insects and berries on them. Each warbler species has its own preferences. Find out what native plants are best for your area. Some common warbler food plants are oak trees, cherry trees, elderberry bushes,

Virginia creeper vines, wild grape vines, mulberry trees, and bayberry bushes.

Water: Birdbaths, streams, and other natural water sources are important. A sprinkler or small dripping hose may give birds a drink. Warblers often take baths by splashing in puddles or fluttering in leaves wet from rain or garden sprinklers.

Shelter: Migrating birds rest in trees, bushes, brush piles, and tangles of vines. They especially like plants near hilltops and along rivers and creeks.

A Place to Raise Young: Warblers need protection wherever they nest. The northern forests are important nesting grounds. Keep dogs from running in wild areas during nesting season, because they may disturb nests on the ground. Fencing cattle to keep them from trampling streamside habitat helps warblers such as yellow warblers and waterthrushes.

Safe Rest Stops: At least 90 million pet cats live in the United States. Migrating warblers land at night. They are tired and often unfamiliar with the neighborhood. They are easy prey for house cats and feral cats. According to Smithsonian scientists, house cats and feral cats kill 1.3 billion to 4 billion birds each year.

Pet cats are a new threat to the warblers' journey, a migration that has been taking place for millions of years. (Pet cats are much more recent arrivals to the continent.) Consider keeping cats indoors year-round, or keep them on a leash or in an enclosure when they are outside. For more information, check out the "Cats Indoors" campaign of American Bird Conservancy: abcbirds.org/program/cats-indoors/.

Air Space: At night, migrating birds are attracted to building lights and become confused, often running into windows. They also collide with cell towers and wind turbines. Speak up for the birds: write letters, make calls, and talk to people in charge about siting towers away from bird migration pathways. Encourage city officials and landowners to participate in Lights Out programs, which turn off lights during bird migration.

Winter Habitat: In the winter, birds need tropical rain forests, tropical dry forests, grasslands, swamps, and mountain forests in Mexico, Central America, South America, and the Caribbean islands. Many also live in shade-grown coffee plantations. This kind of coffee is grown in the shade of trees where birds can live. Other coffee is grown on bare land, in the sun, with no trees overhead; this takes away habitat from warblers and other wild animals. Encourage cafés and coffee drinkers to buy shade-grown coffee when possible. Birds also spend time living in agricultural fields of all kinds; organic farming can help eliminate pesticides that can harm birds. Check with the Nature Conservancy or American Bird Conservancy for ways to support programs that preserve bird habitat all along the migration journey.

Birds We Share

Warblers and other migrating birds cross mountains, oceans, and human political boundaries. These tiny athletes have carried out this incredible migration for millions of years. Their beautiful songs, colorful patterns, and seasonal arrival bring joy to people from Alaska to Peru. Whether you live in North America, South America, or the Caribbean, you can help welcome the warblers and share in this natural connection between diverse habitats, wild birds, and people.

To learn more about warblers, visit these organizations:

American Bird Conservancy
Nonprofit organization that protects summer
and winter habitats for birds, including warblers
abcbirds.org

Cape May Bird Observatory
New Jersey Audubon organization that conducts
warbler (and other bird) research and youth education
birdcapemay.org

Journey North
Education organization that helps students track
seasonal change, including bird migration
learner.org/jnorth/

Mass Audubon
Massachusetts nonprofit that runs education programs,
bird sanctuaries, and nature camps
massaudubon.org

Black Swamp Bird Observatory
Nonprofit that conducts research and education
regarding warblers and other birds
bsbo.org

National Audubon Society
Nonprofit environmental group that
deals with birds in general
audubon.org

To identify the warblers in this book, visit AprilSayre.com.

For Allyn and Bill

Acknowledgments

For twenty-eight years, my husband, Jeff, and I have set aside the first couple weeks of May to celebrate warbler migration. So it's extra special to me that he's joined me by taking some of the photos and reviewing text for this book about our shared love: warblers. We were in the midst of savoring warbler migration at the Biggest Week in American Birding, a festival near Toledo, Ohio, when publisher Allyn Johnston contacted me to say that my long-dreamed book would become real.

Thank you Kimberly Kaufman, executive director of the Black Swamp Bird Observatory, for championing birds and taking time to review this text. Thanks also to Dr. David Toews, postdoctoral associate, Cornell Lab of Ornithology; and Dr. Anna Valdez-Drake, postdoctoral fellow, Department of Forest and Conservation Sciences, University of British Columbia.

For bringing the book to life, thank you Andrea Welch and Lauren "Raindrops" Rille of the Beach Lane team. A special thanks to production manager/texture wizard Elizabeth Blake-Linn for cool covers, year after year. My gratitude to the entire S&S children's book family, especially Jon Anderson, Anne Zafian, Sarah Jane Abbott, Bridget Madsen, and Katharine Wiencke.

Thank you to the scientists, citizen scientists, and volunteers studying warblers and helping support them on their journey. Among these heroes is Harold F. Mayfield, an acclaimed amateur ornithologist who studied the Kirtland's warbler and helped create the plan for habitat protection and cowbird trapping that ultimately kept this bird from extinction.

BEACH LANE BOOKS • An imprint of Simon & Schuster Children's Publishing Division • 1230 Avenue of the Americas, New York, New York 10020 • Copyright © 2018 by April Pulley Sayre • All rights reserved, including the right of reproduction in whole or in part in any form. • BEACH LANE BOOKS is a trademark of Simon & Schuster, Inc. • For information about special discounts for bulk purchases, please contact Simon & Schuster Special Sales at 1-866-506-1949 or business@simonandschuster.com. • The Simon & Schuster Speakers Bureau can bring authors to your live event. For more information or to book an event, contact the Simon & Schuster Speakers Bureau at 1-866-248-3049 or visit our website at www.simonspeakers.com. • Book design by Lauren Rille • The text for this book was set in Adobe Garamond. • Manufactured in China • 1117 SCP • First Edition • 10 9 8 7 6 5 4 3 2 1 • Library of Congress Cataloging-in-Publication Data • Names: Sayre, April Pulley, author, photographer. • Title: Warbler wave / April Pulley Sayre ; photographs by April Pulley Sayre. • Description: First edition. | New York : Beach Lane Books, [2018] | Audience: Age 3–8. | Audience: K to Grade 3. | Includes bibliographical references and index. • Identifiers: LCCN 2017014893 | ISBN 9781481448291 (hardback) | ISBN 9781481448307 (eBook) • Subjects: LCSH: Wood warblers—Migration—Juvenile literature. | Migratory birds—Juvenile literature. | BISAC: JUVENILE FICTION / Animals / Birds. | JUVENILE FICTION / Concepts / Seasons. | JUVENILE FICTION / Nature & the Natural World / General (see also headings under Animals). • Classification: LCC QL696. P2438 S29 2018 | DDC 598.8/721568—dc23 LC record available at https://lccn.loc.gov/2017014893